KT-434-038

25ᵖ

D0319921

For George, Naomi, Felix and Josie.

DUTTON

Published by the Penguin Group
Penguin Books Ltd, 27 Wrights Lane, London W8 5TZ, England
Penguin Books USA Inc., 375 Hudson Street, New York, New York 10014, USA
Penguin Books Australia Ltd, Ringwood, Victoria, Australia
Penguin Books Canada Ltd, 10 Alcorn Avenue, Toronto, Ontario, Canada M4V 3B2
Penguin Books (NZ) Ltd, 182-190 Wairau Road, Auckland 10, New Zealand

Penguin Books Ltd, Registered Offices: Harmondsworth, Middlesex, England

First published 1995
1 3 5 7 9 10 8 6 4 2

Text copyright © Alan Durant, 1995
Illustrations copyright © Nick Schon, 1995

The moral right of the author and illustrator has been asserted

All rights reserved.
Without limiting the rights under copyright reserved above, no part of this
publication may be reproduced, stored in or introduced into a retrieval system, or
transmitted, in any form or by any means (electronic, mechanical, photocopying,
recording or otherwise), without the prior written permission of both the
copyright owner and the above publisher of this book

Manufactured in China by Imago

A CIP catalogue record for this book is available from the British Library

ISBN 0-525-69057-3

Prince Shufflebottom

By Alan Durant Illustrated by Nick Schon

Dutton Children's Books

Everybody loved Prince Bertrand. He had:

curly blond hair,

a little button nose

and an adorable smile.

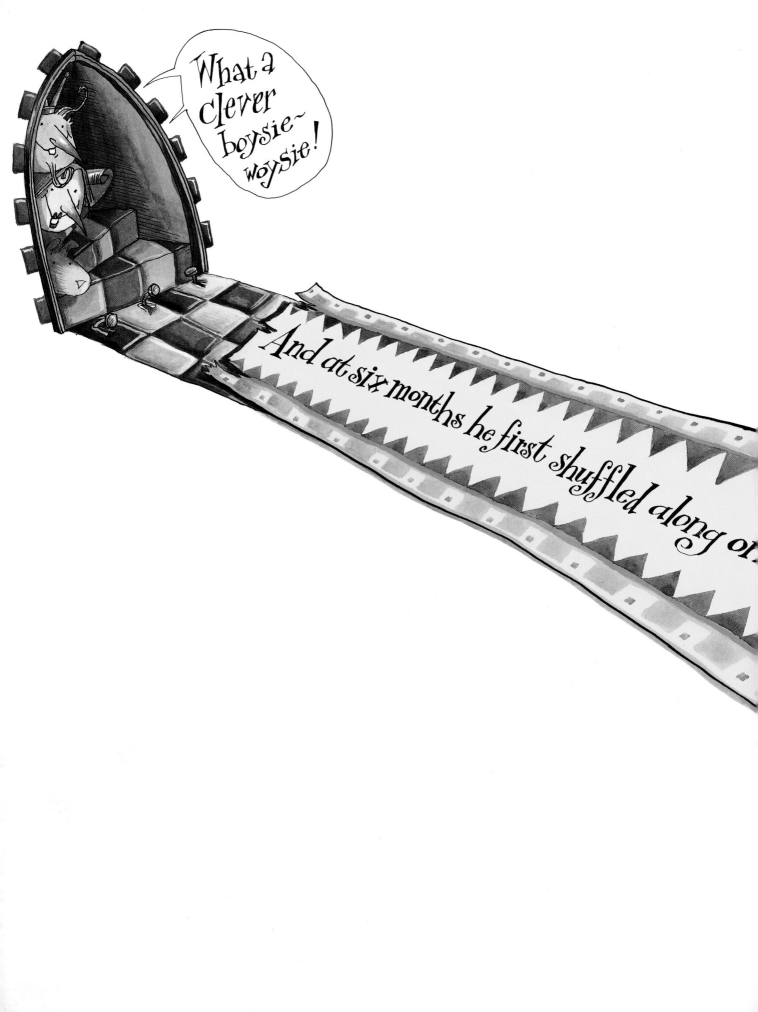

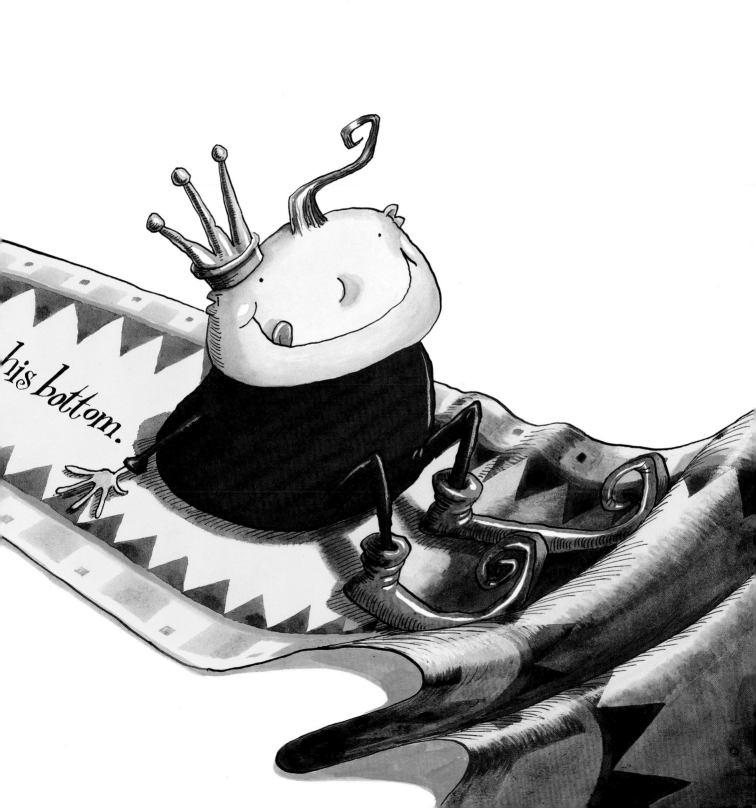

his bottom.

Prince Bertrand shuffled everywhere~round and round and round the nursery, through the corridors,

in and out of rooms,

down the stairs—causing chaos wherever he went.

"Enough is enough," said the King~
and he sent for the Royal Handyman.

"Make me a baby~

"The clever boysie ~ woysie wil

But Prince Bertrand did not like his bag

Royal
Handyman

walker.

He carried on shuffling about the castle ~and around the garden,

where he became great

friends with the gardener's dog.

Months passed.
The King sent for the
Royal Engineer.

Build me a machine that
will make this boy walk,
he ordered.

So the Queen sent for the Royal Cook. "Make me a feast fit for a King," she ordered.

The Royal banqueting table was piled high with cakes and biscuits and chocolates and jellies. Prince Bertrand was left in the room alone.

He shuffled over to the table. "Watch him stand up," whispered the Queen excitedly.

But Prince Bertrand did not stand up. He pulled down the tablecloth instead.

Oh dear, oh dear, sighed the Queen.

Prince Shufflebottom! groaned the King.

Royal Cook

At that moment the gardener's dog came bounding past them into the room

Prince Bertrand reached up
and put his arms on the dog's back.
Then slowly, totteringly,
he pulled himself to his feet and...

ried the King

and Queen.

The castle rang with the joyful news.

Everyone laughed and danced and shouted and cheered.

But no one noticed Prince Bertrand sit down again...

and shuffle away happily with the dog to play in the garden.